CHARLES LINDBERGH

CHARLES LINDBERGH

GROUNDBREAKING AVIATOR

by Rebecca Rowell

Content Consultant:
Kelley A. Welf, Lindbergh Foundation

ABDO
Publishing Company

CREDITS

Published by ABDO Publishing Company, 8000 West 78th Street, Edina, Minnesota 55439. Copyright © 2011 by Abdo Consulting Group, Inc. International copyrights reserved in all countries. No part of this book may be reproduced in any form without written permission from the publisher. The Essential Library™ is a trademark and logo of ABDO Publishing Company.

Printed in the United States of America,
North Mankato, Minnesota
052010
092010

Editor: Amy Van Zee
Copy Editor: Paula Lewis
Interior Design and Production: Kazuko Collins
Cover Design: Kazuko Collins

Library of Congress Cataloging-in-Publication Data
Rowell, Rebecca.
  Charles Lindbergh : groundbreaking aviator / Rebecca Rowell.
     p. cm. — (Essential lives)
  Includes bibliographical references and index.
  ISBN 978-1-61613-516-4
  1. Lindbergh, Charles A. (Charles Augustus), 1902-1974—
Juvenile literature. 2. Air pilots—United States—Biography—
Juvenile literature. I. Title.
  TL540.L5R69 2012
  629.13092—dc22
  [B]
                                    2010000505

TABLE OF CONTENTS

Charles Lindbergh with the Spirit of St. Louis *in 1927*

RISKY JOURNEY

Dark. It was so incredibly dark. Charles Lindbergh had been flying for hours and was nearing his destination. At least he thought he was. The 25-year-old pilot was seated in the cockpit of the *Spirit of St. Louis*, a single-engine plane built specifically for this trip. On this May night in 1927, Lindbergh was looking for Paris. Specifically, he was looking for Le Bourget, the city's airport.

Although he was a young man, Lindbergh was an experienced pilot. He had flown many planes and clocked hundreds of hours in the air. In St. Louis, Missouri, where he worked as an airmail carrier, he was considered an expert flyer. But this flight was different. It was the farthest—and therefore longest—flight he had ever undertaken.

Lindbergh was attempting to cross the Atlantic Ocean without stopping. He was not the first person to attempt the journey. Six men had already died striving to accomplish the feat. Two Frenchmen had failed just days before Lindbergh's scheduled departure. They were flying from Paris to New York, but the duo never made it. Lindbergh was attempting to fly from New York to Paris. He was flying solo, and time would soon reveal his failure or success.

Lindbergh's Competitors

A handful of other pilots shared Lindbergh's goal of being the first to fly across the Atlantic Ocean. In September 1926, René Fonck's plane crashed during takeoff, killing two of his crew members. Richard Byrd's plane crashed during a test flight a month before Lindbergh's departure from New York in 1927. Byrd broke his wrist in the accident. Just ten days later, on April 26, Noel Davis and Stanton Hall Wooster also crashed during a test flight. Both men died. On May 8, Charles Nungesser and François Coli took off from Paris's Le Bourget airfield. The men headed for New York but never made it. They were never seen again.

The Challenge

Lindbergh decided to fly nonstop to Paris in 1927 to win the Orteig Prize. Named for its sponsor, Raymond Orteig, the prize would award $25,000 to the first person to fly from New York City to Paris or from Paris to New York City. Orteig first offered the award in 1919 and made it valid for five years. Aviation was a new field, so crossing the vast Atlantic Ocean nonstop must have seemed an insurmountable task—no one accepted Orteig's challenge. After five years had

Man Learns to Fly

For centuries—long before airplanes existed—humans dreamed of flying. Humans first captured wind for flying kites. The Chinese began flying them circa 400 BCE. In the late fifteenth century, Leonardo da Vinci designed the Ornithopter, an apparatus intended to allow humans to fly. One of Leonardo's other ideas, the helical airscrew, was the predecessor of the helicopter.

In 1783, Joseph and Jacques Montgolfier created the first hot air balloon. On November 21, 1783, the first people traveled in a Montgolfier balloon.

George Cayley continued the development of flight with his gliders during the first half of the nineteenth century. In 1891, Otto Lilienthal designed a glider to carry a passenger. In 1896, Samuel Langley built a model of an airplane that included an engine. He knew power was essential to helping humans fly, but his full-size plane crashed because it was too heavy.

The first airplane took flight in 1903. Orville and Wilbur Wright flew the Wright Flyer for 12 seconds. Following their success, aviation continued to grow, resulting in planes with greater power that could travel higher and over greater distances, including across the Atlantic Ocean.

passed without a single attempt at a transatlantic flight, the French hotel owner extended the challenge another five years.

Aviation was still a new technology, but advancements were being made in the field. Flyers, and those who simply wished they could fly, saw its possibilities. Lindbergh was one such enthusiast. As a young man, Lindbergh attended flying school. Aviation soon became the center of his world. He became a barnstormer who performed flying stunts for audiences and then an airmail pilot. Lindbergh also became an expert at fixing airplanes.

Lindbergh wrote about his decision to pursue the Orteig Prize:

> *Why shouldn't I fly from New York to Paris? I'm almost twenty-five, I have more than four years of aviation behind me, and close to two thousand hours in the air. . . . I've flown my mail through the worst of nights. I know the wind currents of the Rocky Mountains and the storms of the Mississippi Valley as few pilots know them. During my year at Brooks and Kelly as a flying cadet, I learned the basic elements of navigation. . . . Why am I not qualified for such a flight?*[1]

After making the decision to fly nonstop from New York to Paris, Lindbergh also became an airplane designer. He wanted a plane built just for the trip. Lindbergh worked with Ryan Airlines Corporation, in San Diego, California, on the details of his airplane, the *Spirit of St. Louis*. On April 28, 1927, Lindbergh conducted the first of many test flights of his beloved *Spirit of St. Louis*. The young pilot conducted a long test flight on May 10 and May 11 when he flew from San Diego to New York. The trip included a stop in St. Louis and took slightly more than 20 hours. Lindbergh set a transcontinental record. Once in New York, Lindbergh conducted another half dozen test flights. Finally, he was ready for Paris.

The Plane's Name

Lindbergh could not have pursued his dream of flying from New York to Paris without the help of many people. Financial backers in St. Louis, Missouri, where Lindbergh had been living, helped the aviator pay for a custom-designed plane. One of Lindbergh's financial backers suggested the name *Spirit of St. Louis*. Lindbergh used the name in honor of those who paid for the aircraft.

New York to Paris

Lindbergh took off from Roosevelt Field in Long Island, New York, on the morning of May 20, 1927. At the time of departure, the aviator had barely slept at all because of distractions and preparations, and he would stay awake for the entire 30-hour flight. Just as he had dreamed, Lindbergh was attempting to make the first transatlantic flight.

Lindbergh's plane had no front window and no radio. He would use the stars to navigate. He had neither a navigator nor a copilot to rely on for help with flying or keeping him awake. He had decided to fly alone.

But Lindbergh was not alone in his dream. His mother especially encouraged him, and countless citizens worldwide followed his journey with hope. The mechanics who had worked with Lindbergh to build his plane would contribute to and share in the pilot's success. Many Minnesotans cheered on their native son. The Americans who saw the ambitious pilot take off on his risky flight would be eyewitnesses to history, as would the French who awaited his arrival. Thousands of French citizens crammed the airfield to welcome the American flyer. They—and so many others—hoped Lindbergh would not disappoint them.

Emergency Supplies

Lindbergh brought the following emergency supplies with him on his flight to Paris:

- one air raft, with pump and repair kit
- one canteen holding four quarts (3.8 L) of water
- one Armbrust cup (a cup that condenses moisture from breath into drinkable water)
- five cans of army emergency rations
- one hunting knife
- one ball of cord
- one ball of string
- one large needle
- one flashlight
- four red flares, sealed in rubber tubes
- one match safe with matches (a small case to keep matches dry)
- one hacksaw blade

"New York to Paris—it sounds like a dream. . . . Navigation?—over the Atlantic and at night, boring through dark and unknown skies, toward a continent I've never seen? The very thought makes me rise to contend again with the moon—sweeping over oceans and continents, looking down on farms and cities, letting the planet turn below."[2]

—*Charles A. Lindbergh*

The world waited anxiously to learn of Lindbergh's fate. If he succeeded, the young man from a small midwestern town would become known throughout the world. His name and success would forever be etched in history. But disappointing the world was not the aviator's first concern. He simply wanted to complete his flight. All Charles Lindbergh needed was some light to pierce the dark. —

Charles Lindbergh was a talented and determined aviator.

Charles Lindbergh circa 1902, with his mother, Evangeline

Young Charles

Charles Augustus Lindbergh was born on February 4, 1902, in Detroit, Michigan. His parents lived in Little Falls, Minnesota, where his father had established successful businesses in both law and real estate. But Evangeline Lindbergh wanted to give birth to her first child in her hometown in Michigan. Her husband, Charles August—commonly known as C. A.—helped Evangeline get settled into her parents' home at the end of January. He then returned home to attend to business for a few weeks, planning to travel back to Michigan for the birth of the couple's first child. But the baby arrived sooner than expected, and C. A. missed the birth. Five weeks after Charles was born, Evangeline returned to Little Falls with her newborn son. C. A.'s two daughters from a previous marriage also lived with them in their small town in central Minnesota.

THE LINDBERGH FARM

The 800-mile (1,290-km) trip to Little Falls brought Evangeline to a new home on the couple's farm by the Mississippi River. The house reflected C. A.'s success. Evangeline

Evangeline Lodge Land Lindbergh

Evangeline Lodge Land was born in Detroit, Michigan, in 1876. After graduating from the University of Michigan, she accepted a teaching position in Little Falls, Minnesota. There, she met C. A. Lindbergh. The widower was 17 years her senior and the father of two girls.

C. A. and Evangeline married in March 1901. She gave birth to her first and only child, Charles, less than a year later. Evangeline was devoted to her son but was never much of a mother to her stepdaughters. They were sent to boarding school and to live with other family members. When Charles went off to college, Evangeline resumed teaching, which she continued to do until 1942. She died in 1954.

had a cook and a maid to help around the house. There was also a foreman who lived on the farm and oversaw a handful of workers.

The Lindberghs' home was lavish. Most residents of Little Falls and the surrounding area had far less money. These neighbors did not live with many of the niceties that the Lindberghs could easily afford, such as Oriental rugs and mahogany bookcases. But the Lindberghs lost their beautiful house to a fire in 1905. A new, smaller house was built on the previous foundation.

By 1905, an election was nearing. Many locals wanted new representation in Washington DC. Many of them believed C. A. Lindbergh would be a good choice to represent them. The senior Lindbergh was elected to the U.S. Congress in 1906. From this time until 1917, young Charles spent only summers on the family farm. When

The Lindbergh House

The Lindberghs' second home is now a historical site maintained by the Minnesota Historical Society. Visitors can see burn marks on the wood floors where Charles kept incubators to hatch chickens. The kitchen floor has marks from when Charles chopped wood for the stove.

they were together in Little Falls, C. A. and Charles enjoyed all that rural Minnesota had to offer, including hunting in nearby woods and swimming in the Mississippi River.

LOVE OF NATURE AND ANIMALS

Thanks to his rural surroundings and his father, Charles developed a love for nature early in life. His earliest memories included seeing and hearing the Mississippi River while in his crib near a window. The river was very much a part of the boy's life. He wrote

Swedish Roots

Charles Lindbergh's father, C. A. Lindbergh, was a Swedish immigrant. His father, Ola Månsson, had been a politician in Sweden and had been convicted of embezzlement. Månsson was married and had children; he also had a mistress. She was C. A.'s mother. After Månsson's political career suffered because of the conviction, he decided to move to the United States to start a new life. He asked his wife and children to join him, but they declined. Månsson and his mistress, Lovisa Callén, headed for Minnesota, a popular destination for Scandinavian immigrants during the nineteenth century.

The family's journey began with a three-day trip across the North Sea to England. Then, they traveled by train to Liverpool and boarded a ship that would take a month to reach Quebec, Canada. The family crossed the U.S. border into Michigan by train and headed to Iowa. In Dubuque, they boarded a boat on the Mississippi River and traveled north to Minnesota. The family settled near Melrose. By this time, the family had new names. Ola and Lovisa became August and Louise Carline Lindbergh. Two of Ola's sons had changed their last names to Lindbergh while attending the University of Lund in Sweden, and Ola used the same name. The baby was named Charles August Lindbergh.

of sleeping as close to nature as he could: "I would sleep on the screened porch overlooking the river. There I was in close contact with sun, wind, rain, and stars."[1]

School

Charles did not begin school until he was eight years old. Until that time, Evangeline tutored her son. Once he began a formal education, he never spent much time at one school because of his frequent moves between his father's home in Washington DC, his mother's family's home in Detroit, and his parents' home in Little Falls. His first school was the Force School in Washington DC. The experience was not a pleasant one for young Charles:

[I was] forced to sit still in a strange room, amid strange children, and surrounded by strange and unknown conventions . . . [I remember] countless hours of sitting at a desk . . . waiting, waiting, waiting for the school to close.[2]

Not Junior

Charles Augustus Lindbergh was named after his father, but not exactly. He is not a junior. C. A. is Charles August. Evangeline Lindbergh gave her son's middle name an extra syllable, making him Charles Augustus.

Charles Augustus Lindbergh and his father, C. A., circa 1910

Charles went on to attend other schools. In
Detroit, Charles never completed a full year of
school because he began late and left early. In
Washington DC, he managed to spend two years
at the Sidwell Friends School, but his experience

there was an unhappy one because children made
fun of his last name. Playing off the name of a foul-
smelling cheese, they called him
"Limburger" and "Cheesy."

An Intellectual Heritage

Charles's experiences in
Detroit were different
from those in Little Falls
and Washington DC.
In Michigan, he culti-
vated an appreciation for
inquiry from his maternal
grandfather, Charles Land,
who was a dentist and an
inventor. Land developed
porcelain crowns for
teeth and created an air
purification system for his
family's house.

When Charles was
with his father, he heard
philosophical, political,
and social discussions.
With his grandfather and
the rest of the Land fam-
ily, Charles was exposed
to scientific debate and
developed an appre-
ciation for science and
discovery. These early
experiences shaped Lind-
bergh and his lifetime
interests and endeavors.

GREAT ADVENTURES

While the frequent moving
brought regular upheaval to young
Charles's life, it also brought
opportunities to explore the world.
One of these opportunities would
set his mind on a path to flying.
During the summer of 1912,
C. A. Lindbergh arranged for
Evangeline and Charles to attend
the Aeronautical Trials at Fort Myer,
Virginia.

The trials included several
airplanes. Young Charles watched
them being tuned up. He then saw
one in action. It was a moment that
would stay with him. He later wrote:

> *Then one of the planes took off and raced
> a motor car around the oval track in*

*front of us. You could see its pilot clearly, out in front—pants'
legs flapping, and cap visor pointed backward to streamline
in the wind.*[3]

Mother and son also watched the planes attack an
imaginary battleship. While flying over an outline of
a ship that had been drawn in chalk, the pilots threw
oranges at their target below. What Charles saw at
Fort Myer made him want to become a pilot.

EARLY GRADUATION

In 1914, the United States began fighting in
the Great War, which later became known as World
War I. In 1918, Charles left high school in Little Falls
to help the war effort.

Sixteen-year-old Charles took over the family
farm. His high school allowed students to earn
school credit toward graduation by raising food
for the war. With the help of a man his father had
hired, Charles ran the entire farm. He built and
fixed housing for the animals, milked cows, plowed
the fields, and raised chickens. It was hard work,
but Charles succeeded. He earned enough credit
to graduate from high school, and he collected his
diploma from Little Falls High on June 5, 1918.

Charles continued to manage the farm until 1920. Now 18, Charles decided to continue his education and needed to focus on preparing for college. He passed on the management of the farm to tenant workers. It was time for the next stage of his life. New adventures were on the horizon. ⌒

The Nonpartisan Leader

MAY 6, 1918

CHARLES A. LINDBERGH
FARMER-LABOR CANDIDATE FOR GOVERNOR OF MINNESOTA

Beginning a New Series — "The Sniffing Bloodhounds of the Press."
Read It and Learn Why the Newspapers Fight the Farmers.

A 1918 campaign advertisement for C. A. Lindbergh. Charles Lindbergh spent much of his youth traveling due to his father's political career.

Charles Lindbergh, back right, and members of the ROTC rifle team at the University of Wisconsin–Madison

DREAMING OF FLIGHT

After completing high school, Charles Lindbergh was ready to move on to college. When selecting a school, he focused mostly on location. Lindbergh entered the University of Wisconsin's Madison campus in the fall of 1920 to study mechanical engineering. He wrote later that he "finally chose the University of Wisconsin—probably more because of its nearby lakes than because of its high engineering standards."[1]

His departure for school marked the end of an era in Little Falls. Lindbergh wrote that going off to college "ended all my close contacts with our farm. I returned on several occasions, both in winter and summer, but never for many days at a time."[2]

University of Wisconsin–Madison

The first building on the University of Wisconsin–Madison campus opened to students in 1851, and two students were its first graduates in 1854. Initially, the university was open only to men, but women began being admitted in 1863.

The public university has grown considerably since being established. Today, the University of Wisconsin–Madison has approximately 40,000 students from across the nation and around the world.

College and ROTC

Although he was curious and loved to explore and learn, Lindbergh did not enjoy studying. Rather than focusing on academics, the freshman spent considerable time pursuing outdoor activities. He enjoyed riding his motorcycle and wanted to see how far he could jump it into a nearby lake. Some friends talked him out of actually finding out.

Lindbergh also liked to shoot guns, which was something he began doing at a very young age. He was good with both pistols and rifles, and his skill garnered him positions on the university's shooting teams. He was an outstanding marksman who regularly shot bull's-eyes.

Lindbergh's Motorcycle

While still working on the family farm, Lindbergh bought a motorcycle. He rode it frequently and became a skilled motorcyclist and mechanic. When he went off to college in 1920, he drove himself, riding his beloved motorcycle to Madison.

Lindbergh's marksmanship proved advantageous in other campus activities. During his freshman year, the young man joined the Reserve Officers' Training Corps (ROTC). This program trains students who are attending colleges and universities to become officers in the United States military. The program proved to be what interested Lindbergh most at the university. He wrote of his participation, "On days for ROTC training we wore our uniforms at all classes—proudly."[3] As a cadet, Lindbergh not only practiced shooting, he studied guns and trajectory. He also learned about leadership. After years of not fitting in with classmates, Lindbergh finally felt like part of a group.

This feeling continued into the summer following his freshman year, when Lindbergh traveled to Kentucky to fulfill part of the requirements of being a cadet. He spent six weeks at

Camp Knox completing artillery training. Although his time there was regimented, which was quite a change from the adventurous life he was accustomed to, Lindbergh thrived. He wrote of his experience:

> *I learned to know the imperative note and thrill of the bugle. We rose early, worked hard, slept soundly. The strictness of discipline amazed me, but I enjoyed it, and realized its value in military life.*[4]

Although he fared quite well as an ROTC cadet and a member of the university's shooting squads, Lindbergh mostly floundered as a student. He was put on probation during his first term. Lindbergh recognized that he needed to focus on his studies to become a successful

Leaving the Farm to Fly

When Lindbergh moved to Madison, Wisconsin, to attend college, he would never live in Little Falls regularly again. The same became true for his mother. When her son decided on the University of Wisconsin, Evangeline Lindbergh decided to move to the college town as well. She arrived in Madison before Charles and found an apartment near campus for the two of them. To make it feel like home, Evangeline had items shipped from Little Falls.

Lindbergh had many fond memories of his hometown. He wrote about returning to Little Falls just a few years after leaving:

And after buying my first plane in Georgia in the spring of 1923, I barnstormed west to Texas and then north to Little Falls, landing near the old log buildings on the western forty of our farm. . . . I felt nostalgia then if I ever felt it in my life, for I knew the farming days I loved so much were over. I had made my choice. I loved still more to fly.[5]

student, but he did not follow through. He missed the first day of classes of the new term. Before long, Lindbergh was exploring possibilities other than college.

Tall and Thin

Lindbergh needed to pass a physical exam and to be fitted for a uniform when he joined the ROTC at the University of Wisconsin–Madison. The 18-year-old Lindbergh was long and lean. He was six feet two inches (1.9 m) tall and a mere 148 pounds (67 kg). He passed the exam, but the local tailor who measured the teen for a uniform was a bit surprised by Lindbergh's thin arms.

Flying School

Lindbergh had become enamored with flying when he was a young boy. His interest grew as he kept up with the events of the war. He read about the extensive aerial combat in Europe and the war's flying aces: René Fonck from France, Eddie Rickenbacker from the United States, and Manfred von Richtofen from Germany— the great Red Baron, the war's top ace. Lindbergh decided to pursue his dream of flying.

By the winter of 1921–1922, Lindbergh was contacting flying schools. Two offered courses that would begin in April 1922: Nebraska Aircraft Corporation, located in Lincoln, and Ralph C. Diggins School of Aeronautics in Chicago, Illinois. Lindbergh shared his dream of flying with some friends. They discouraged him from dropping out of college. But leaving the University of Wisconsin soon became more than an option. His father was broke, which made supporting his wife and son in Madison impossible. Furthermore, the young man's consistently poor grades eventually prompted the university to ask Lindbergh to leave.

In March 1922, Lindbergh hopped on his motorcycle and headed to Lincoln, Nebraska. He chose to study there because the training involved more than just learning to pilot a plane. Students were taught about all aspects of airplanes and flying, including building and maintaining the machines. The school also advertised that it helped students find work. Lindbergh arrived in Lincoln on April 1. Two days later, he showed up for his first day of training as a pilot.

The school was not quite what Lindbergh had pictured. The business had changed hands since Lindbergh had sent his application. Now named Lincoln Standard Aircraft, the flying school had been neglected in the turnover. But the new owner, Ray "Skipper" Page, accepted Lindbergh's tuition payment and put the lanky young man to work.

Lindbergh's hands-on training fit well with his style of learning. Page immediately started Lindbergh on taking apart motors. The trainee also had the task of varnishing fabric that would form a plane's fuselage and wings. The treatment helped waterproof and strengthen the material. Lindbergh also reconditioned planes, which included converting cockpits from single to double occupancy. Lindbergh loved the work, which he told his mother in a letter, writing, "So far I have had work that is not very exciting, but interesting to *me*."[6] The following week, Lindbergh experienced his first plane ride.

Throughout April, Lindbergh studied all aspects of an airplane. He also began flying and proved to be a natural at it, though landing was challenging. By the end of his second month, Lindbergh's instructor deemed him ready for his first solo flight. Lindbergh had logged only eight hours of training in the cockpit. But Page would not allow Lindbergh to fly solo without a $500 bond to cover any damage that might occur while Lindbergh was at the helm. Without money to pay for the bond and without enough experience to be hired as a pilot, Lindbergh had to think of another way to acquire the training he so desired.

Charles Lindbergh admired World War I pilot Eddie Rickenbacker.

Charles Lindbergh set his sights on becoming a pilot in the early 1920s.

FINALLY, A PILOT

R ay Page was in the process of selling
Lincoln Standard Aircraft's training
plane to Erold G. Bahl when Lindbergh was ready
to fly solo in spring 1922. Bahl, a top pilot in the
area, worked as a barnstormer. He traveled around

performing for crowds, flying stunts, providing exhibitions, and even taking people on flights. Bahl's next stop was southeastern Nebraska. Lindbergh thought accompanying Bahl on his tour would provide much-needed experience and training, so he offered to assist Bahl for free. Bahl agreed.

Lindbergh was charged with cleaning the plane and drumming up business. He had to convince people to spend their money to see the show or take a flight. Lindbergh did well—and better than Bahl expected. The aspiring aviator suggested to Bahl that they might draw a bigger crowd by having a wing walker. Lindbergh was soon riding the plane's wing as Bahl piloted the craft.

Lindbergh flew back to Lincoln with Bahl in June 1922. Lindbergh wanted to purchase his own plane and needed money. He worked in Page's aircraft factory earning $15 per week. Eager to continue and expand his barnstorming experience, Lindbergh acquired a new skill to excite crowds.

LINDBERGH THE JUMPER

Charles and Kathryn Hardin were parachute makers whom Page hired to work at his factory. The couple was also part of Page's Aerial Pageant, in which Charles Hardin was dropped from an airplane wing 2,000 feet (610 m) in the air. Lindbergh asked Hardin to teach him how to jump. However, young Lindbergh wanted to try a double jump. For this trick, the jumper wears two parachutes. The first opens, but he intentionally lets it go. The jumper relies on a second chute to float him safely to the ground. Loss of the first chute would certainly excite any crowd.

Lindbergh made his first jump on an evening

Barnstorming

Barnstorming was popular during the 1920s. Stunt pilots and aerialists traveled around the rural United States. They performed for paying crowds and thrilled onlookers with death-defying acts. Popular stunts for pilots included spins and dives. Aerialists would walk on the wings, parachute off the plane, and walk from one plane to another in midair.

Barnstormers performed solo and in groups. A pilot would fly over a town to attract attention and then land at a farm in the area. After negotiating with the farmer to use his field for the show, the barnstormer would fly over the town again to drop handbills. The announcements let people know about the show, which often included airplane rides and daredevil performances—all for a small fee. Excited townspeople would follow the plane to the performance field. Larger groups of barnstormers formed to create flying circuses. These groups sometimes had promoters who would organize shows in advance.

Lindbergh's skills and sense of adventure made him a great barnstormer and aerialist. By the time Lindbergh left for Paris in 1927, the practice of barnstorming had begun to decline. New safety regulations established by the U.S. government made plane upkeep difficult and some forms of stunts illegal.

in June. He was 1,800 feet (549 m) in the air. As planned, his first parachute opened, which he then detached. The second chute did not immediately open. Lindbergh was hurtling headfirst to the ground. But he did not panic. The second chute opened, and Lindbergh landed safely.

DAREDEVIL AND MECHANIC

Lindbergh's skills as a wing walker and parachute jumper made him quite popular. Bahl wanted to keep Lindbergh as an assistant, but this time he would pay the young man. Page wanted to keep Lindbergh as a factory employee. Pilot and barnstormer H. J. Lynch and his business partner "Banty" Rogers wanted Lindbergh to jump at events in Kansas and Colorado. Lindbergh agreed, but not before obtaining a new parachute from Charles Hardin.

Lindbergh traveled by train to Kansas, where he began a two-month stint traveling the land and skies of Kansas, Nebraska, Colorado, and Wyoming. He used all of his recently acquired skills as a wing walker, a skydiver, and a mechanic.

Barnstormers performed exciting aerial stunts for crowds.

"Jenny"

The barnstorming season ended in October, leaving Lindbergh in Montana. During his trip back to Lincoln, Nebraska, the daredevil made a decision. He would have his own plane by the following spring.

That winter, Charles visited his father several times. During these visits, C. A. Lindbergh realized his son's interest in aviation was not simply a passing fancy. And though the older Lindbergh was struggling financially, he agreed to become his son's business partner and help him buy a plane.

Charles Lindbergh headed to Americus, Georgia, in April 1923. He was told that Souther Field, located near Americus, offered good deals on airplanes. Souther Field had aircraft and parts from the war. Lindbergh settled into barracks at Souther Field and studied the available stock. He also negotiated owner John Wyche down to half the usual price of $1,000 for a plane.

Lindbergh chose a Curtiss JN4-D, known as a Jenny. The biplane seated two people and was used for training during the war. In addition to the plane, Lindbergh bought a brand-new engine and an extra 20-gallon (76-L) gas tank. He also paid for a paint job.

Lindbergh stayed at Souther Field for two weeks while his plane was being readied. When the mechanic working on the plane was finished, Lindbergh took the Jenny for a test flight. This was his first solo flight. He struggled to get the plane off the ground and landed after reaching a height of only four feet (1.2 m).

Flying Solo

Charles Lindbergh said of his first solo flight, "No matter how much training you've had, your first solo is far different from all other flights. You are completely independent, hopelessly beyond help, entirely responsible, and terribly alone in space."[1]

He was embarrassed, but he knew that aborting his takeoff was better than risking a crash.

But Lindbergh did not quit. A young flyer named Henderson joined Lindbergh in the plane and guided him through several takeoffs and landings. Later that spring day in 1923, Lindbergh finally achieved what he had been longing for: a successful solo flight. During the year after his decision to become a pilot, Lindbergh had studied planes inside and out. He had worked as a wing walker and a skydiver. Now, finally, he had become a pilot.

ARMY CADET

Lindbergh continued to barnstorm. He moved back to Minnesota to do so in his home state. In the summer of 1923, while barnstorming in southern Minnesota, Lindbergh was approached by a young man who

Campaigning by Plane

After learning to fly and returning to Minnesota to visit his father, Lindbergh helped C. A. campaign for an open senate seat in June 1923. He told C. A. how easy it would be to cover an entire town with campaign literature. Charles and his father climbed into the plane's cockpit. Son would fly while father would drop handbills out the plane's window. But C. A. did something his son did not expect. The pilot wrote later, "It did not occur to me that he might throw them out all at once, but he did, and the thick stack of sheets struck the stabilizer with a thud."[2] The plane was not damaged, but the literature did not get far.

suggested the pilot enlist in the Army Air Corps. As a flying cadet, he could fly the newest and most powerful aircraft available. This appealed greatly to Lindbergh.

Lindbergh enlisted. He had several months before he needed to report to Brooks Field in San Antonio, Texas. Lindbergh spent the time barnstorming in the Midwest, including Minnesota, Wisconsin, and Illinois. He attended the St. Louis Air Meet in Missouri in early October. He also became a flight instructor and taught a few students.

Lindbergh reported to Brooks Field on March 15, 1924, to begin training as an army cadet. The 22-year-old was one of 104 cadets, many of whom would be eliminated from the rigorous program.

Lindbergh immersed himself in the books and hands-on training required of his new role. He flew aircraft that were more powerful than his own. He was in school again, but

The Death of C. A. Lindbergh

While Charles Lindbergh was a cadet in Texas, he received sad news. A telegram on April 23, 1924, reported that his father, C. A. Lindbergh, had taken ill and was in a hospital in Rochester, Minnesota. The elder Lindbergh's health was declining rapidly. He was diagnosed with a brain tumor. Charles Lindbergh took leave to visit his father. It would be the last time Charles would see his father alive. Lindbergh returned to training to avoid being kicked out of the program. On May 24, he received another telegram. His father had died.

the experience felt new. This time he cared about his studies and wanted to succeed. And he did succeed, but not without incident.

During training, his plane and another cadet's plane bumped. The two men had to jump out into the air before their crafts crashed. The two cadets survived. A few weeks earlier, two cadets had crashed and died, so Lindbergh and the other cadet were fortunate that they survived the midair collision. A little more than a week later, Lindbergh graduated at the top of his class. By that time, the number of cadets had dwindled from 104 to 18. Upon graduating in March 1925, Lindbergh was commissioned as a second lieutenant in the U.S. Army Air Service Reserve. More flying awaited the young, determined pilot. ⌐

Nicknames

Nicknames were common for cadets. Lindbergh had several, some of which he acquired before joining the U.S. Army. He was known as Slim because of his build. Charlie and Carl were derivations of his given name. Old Swede reflected his heritage.

*Enlisting in the Army Air Corps helped Charles Lindbergh
learn about aviation.*

Charles Lindbergh at Lambert Field in 1925

Working as a Flyer

In spring 1925, Second Lieutenant
Lindbergh was looking for work. He
had applied for a position in the regular Army Air
Service but had not yet been offered one. Now, the
23-year-old was free to look for nonmilitary work.

Lindbergh turned down an employment offer in Georgia as a crop duster spraying fields from his plane because the pay was too low. He then headed to St. Louis, Missouri.

Lindbergh had been to St. Louis before and liked the city. He rented a room at a boarding house near the 170-acre (69-ha) Lambert Field, where Major Albert Bond Lambert had trained balloon pilots during World War I. St. Louis would prove to be an excellent choice for Lindbergh.

Lindbergh did not have to wait long before receiving another job offer. Frank and William Robertson were pilots who had flown in the war. They owned and operated Robertson Aircraft Corporation. The brothers wanted Lindbergh to be their chief airmail pilot. However, the Robertson Aircraft Corporation had not yet been granted the St. Louis to Chicago route and had to wait for approval from the U.S. Postal Service. Lindbergh agreed to accept the position if it became available. However, he still needed work in the meantime.

Miscellaneous Flying

Lindbergh had no problem filling his days while waiting to hear if Robertson Aircraft would run the mail between St. Louis and Chicago. He spent a lot of time at nearby Lambert Field. He took on flying students and transported passengers short distances. Daredevil Lindbergh also made a return to barnstorming for a few weeks in Illinois, Iowa, and Missouri. Lindbergh often created his own work, but he continued to receive offers as well.

In May 1925, the eager flyer was asked to take part in Vera May Dunlap's Flying Circus. Lindbergh wowed the crowd in Illinois with his flying. Spectators were amazed by his ability to survive

St. Louis

St. Louis, Missouri, is located in the middle of the United States. The city sits by the Mississippi River just south of where it meets the Missouri River. St. Louis was founded as a trading post by French fur traders in 1764. They named the location after King Louis IX of France, who reigned during the thirteenth century. The site became headquarters of the fur trade and a stopping point for both traders and explorers. St. Louis was formally incorporated as a town in 1809. In 1822, it became a city.

As the fur trade decreased, St. Louis relied on the river for its success. Manufacturing and shipping increased, and the railroad brought new residents to the prospering city. In 20 years, from 1840 to 1860, the population grew from 16,469 to 160,773. Immigrants from Germany, Ireland, and Eastern Europe joined African Americans who had moved northward. Today, St. Louis is an important port and freight rail stop.

Perhaps the most recognizable feature of the city is its Gateway Arch, which was completed in 1965 to honor St. Louis as a gateway to the western United States during the nineteenth century.

when the plane's engine stopped 3,000 feet (914 m) in the air. Lindbergh even landed with the engine turned off.

Back at Lambert Field in St. Louis, Lindbergh accepted another offer. He became a test pilot. On June 2, Lindbergh climbed into an OXX-6 Plywood Special. It was a new, four-passenger plane intended for commercial use. The plane did not respond well to all of the tests Lindbergh put it through. In particular, the plane would not spin as it should, and then it would not respond at all. The aircraft began to plummet. Only a few hundred feet above the ground, Lindbergh managed to clear the cockpit and parachute to the ground. He described the event: "The ground was right there, leaping at me. Trees and houses looked tremendous. There seemed scarcely enough room for a parachute to string out."[1]

Although the plane crashed, Lindbergh escaped unharmed. After spending two weeks fulfilling his Air Service Reserve duties, the second lieutenant returned to civilian flying. This time, he took on work in Denver with the promise of receiving a salary of $400 per month. He joined the Mil-Hi Airways and Flying Circus. As usual, Lindbergh readily took on daredevil flying. With the barnstorming season ending in the fall, the pilot headed back to St. Louis, where he spent the winter of 1925–1926 as a test pilot and an instructor. Some of Lindbergh's teaching was for the Missouri National Guard, in which he enlisted and attended weekly drills. He also was busy planning the airmail route from St. Louis to Chicago. The Robertson brothers had won the contract, and Lindbergh was preparing to be an airmail pilot.

Airmail

Robertson Aircraft Corporation had a new hangar, five planes, and Lindbergh as its chief pilot. He had a lot to do before the first piece of mail could be delivered. First, Lindbergh needed additional pilots, so he hired Phil Love and Thomas Nelson to also fly the route in separate planes. Second, Lindbergh had to plot the course from St. Louis to Chicago. He decided on nine landing fields along

"I've never chosen the safer branches of aviation. I've followed adventure, not safety. I've flown for the love of flying, done the things I wanted most to do. . . . Why should man want to fly at all? . . . What justifies the risk of life? . . . I believe the risks I take are justified by the sheer love of the life I lead."[2]

—Charles A. Lindbergh

the route, which was approximately 280 miles (451 km). These were not designated airfields but simply fields in which a plane could land.

After all of the waiting and careful planning, Lindbergh flew the first flight on the airmail route on April 15, 1926. It would be the first of many, as Robertson's contract was for five round-trip flights each week.

But even with the most careful and diligent planning, problems arose. Weather can cause challenges for pilots. Lindbergh struggled with dense fog during a night flight to Chicago on September 26. He simply could not find the airfield and eventually ran out of fuel. He had to jump from the cockpit. He was not hurt, although the plane came uncomfortably close to him in the air. Initially, Lindbergh and the farmer who found him in a field could not find the plane, but someone spotted it two miles (3.2 km) away. The farmer drove Lindbergh to the crash site, where the pilot rescued the sacks of mail from the cockpit. He got them on a train for delivery to Chicago. Six weeks later, Lindbergh lost another plane while delivering mail. Again, the weather was a problem. And again, he walked away unharmed.

*Charles Lindbergh's airmail plane crashed in 1926,
but Lindbergh was not hurt.*

Startling Thought

The cockpit provided solitude and surroundings conducive to letting Lindbergh's mind wander—

even to seemingly wild possibilities.
During a 1926 flight to Chicago, he
had an exciting idea as he transported
mail to the city, just as he did
every week. He thought about the
possibilities of aircraft and flight.
He considered the Bellanca, a plane
more advanced than his own. With
modifications that allowed for more
fuel than is usually carried, the plane
could travel a great distance:

> *In a Bellanca filled with fuel tanks I could
> fly on all night, like the moon. How far
> could it go if it carried nothing but
> gasoline? . . . It's fast, too. . . . Possibly—
> my mind is startled at its thought—I
> could fly nonstop between New York and
> Paris. . . .*

> *Not so long ago, when I was a student
> in college, just flying an airplane seemed
> a dream. But that dream turned into
> reality. . . . Why wouldn't a flight across
> the ocean prove as possible as all these
> things have been? As I attempted them,*

Favored by the Angels

The story of Lindbergh's
second crash of an air-
mail plane was printed in
newspapers. Afterward,
the pilot received a let-
ter from Sergeant August
W. Theimann, who had
served with Lindbergh
in the Army Air Ser-
vice. Theimann wrote, "I
don't know whether you
possess any angelistic
instinct, but it appears
to me as though you are
favored by the angels."[3]

I can - - - I will attempt that too. I'll organize a flight to Paris![4]

The pilot soon set out in pursuit of his dream. ⌐

Plan of Attack

When Lindbergh decided he would attempt to make the New York–Paris flight, he created a plan for accomplishing his goal. He divided his plan into seven categories: action, advantages, results, cooperation, equipment, maps, and landmarks. He divided the first category, "action," into eight subcategories: plan, propaganda, backers, equipment, cooperation of manufacturers, accessory information, point of departure, and advertising. Lindbergh listed two possible results for his plan: success and failure.

Charles Lindbergh carefully planned his transatlantic flight.

By the fall of 1926, Charles Lindbergh was a successful pilot.

New York to Paris

n the fall of 1926, Charles Lindbergh could not get the idea of flying to Paris, France, out of his mind. But other experienced pilots also set out to be the first to fly across the Atlantic Ocean. On September 14, René Fonck attempted the flight. He never made it into the air because his plane burst into flames during takeoff. Fonck and his copilot survived, but two crew members died.

Lindbergh used Fonck's accident as a learning opportunity. Lindbergh questioned what could have been done differently and considered how he would have approached the flight. For example, Lindbergh believed the four people in the Fonck crew was three too many. He also thought the plane could have carried different items. Despite Fonck's failure, Lindbergh was not deterred. He considered several factors, the most important of which was the plane. He needed to get one.

Finding Backers

Lindbergh wanted to buy a plane for his planned transatlantic flight, but planes were expensive. He thought the Bellanca model airplane might work well, but it cost at least $10,000. Lindbergh had money in savings, but not nearly enough to buy a Bellanca.

He decided to seek out St. Louis businessmen to back his venture. Lindbergh knew several such men from flying and instructing them, including

a banker and a broker. Lindbergh believed these
men would be willing to finance him if he offered to
repay them with the $25,000 Orteig Prize he would
receive after reaching Paris. In addition, the backers
would own his plane. They would also benefit from
the attention Lindbergh's success would bring to
St. Louis.

Lindbergh put together a prospectus detailing his
idea. He would present it to potential backers. He
took his plan to Harry Hall Knight, a broker. Knight
contacted Harold Bixby, who was the vice president
of a bank. The two men agreed to raise $15,000 for
Lindbergh. In all, there were nine St. Louis backers.

Ryan Airlines

With Knight and Bixby overseeing finances for
Lindbergh's project, the pilot could
now focus on finding a plane. He
had looked previously, but without
success. Some planes were simply too
expensive. Some companies refused
to let Lindbergh take their crafts on
what they deemed a doomed flight.

Lindbergh contacted Ryan
Airlines on February 3, 1927.

Focus on the Flight

Harry Hall Knight was
eager to back Charles
Lindbergh's transatlantic
flight. He told Lindbergh,
"Slim, you ought not to
be running around worry-
ing about raising money.
You've got to put all your
attention on that flight if
you're going to make it."[1]

The California company responded the following day. Ryan Airlines could create a monoplane for Lindbergh similar to one already in production. It would take three months and cost $6,000 without an engine. Lindbergh pursued other possible planes and makers but to no avail.

While Lindbergh was busy trying to find a plane for his trip, other aviators were doing the same. Lindbergh was not the only pilot intent on being the first to fly across the Atlantic and winning the Orteig Prize. Noel Davis and Stanton H. Wooster were planning on flying together. Lindbergh was eager to get a plane and get going.

On February 23, Lindbergh traveled to San Diego, California, to meet with Ryan Airlines. Lindbergh and Donald Hall, the company's chief engineer, were of the same mind regarding the plane. The plane, with an engine, would cost $10,580. Lindbergh contacted his backers, who agreed with the deal. Lindbergh placed his order the following day and immediately began designing the plane with Hall. The two worked with a single goal in mind: get to Paris. To do this, the plane would have extra fuel tanks. To accommodate the increased weight, the wingspan would be longer.

The *Spirit of St. Louis* was completed on April 28, a little more than two months after it was ordered. Lindbergh immediately took it for the first of several test flights. His last test was May 4. Less than a week later, on May 10, Lindbergh headed east, stopping in St. Louis on his way to New York.

Specs

The *Spirit of St. Louis* was a custom-built craft created by Ryan Airlines with guidance and considerable input from Lindbergh. Donald Hall, a Ryan employee, designed the craft, which was based on the company's Ryan M-2. The plane's specifications were as follows:

- Wingspan: 46 feet (14 m)
- Length: 27 feet 8 inches (8 m)
- Height: 9 feet 10 inches (3 m)
- Weight (empty): 2,150 pounds (975 kg)
- Engine: Wright Whirlwind J-5C, 223 horsepower

CHASING THE DREAM

After spending the night in St. Louis, Lindbergh headed for New York. He landed at Long Island's Curtiss Field on the morning of May 12. He spent the next several days preparing for his flight to Paris and waiting for the weather to clear. Finally, departure was just hours away. Lindbergh was staying at a local hotel and wanted only to sleep before his high-profile flight. But there were too many interruptions for him to get the rest he so desired.

Just before 8:00 on the morning of May 20, 1927, Lindbergh took off from New York's Roosevelt Field. He was headed to Paris, more than

3,600 miles (5,794 km) away. He flew without sleep in challenging weather and without a companion or a radio. He did have the stars, which he used to navigate. The stars, his planning, and his beloved plane served him well.

Thirty-three hours after leaving New York City, Lindbergh neared his final destination. It was night, and Lindbergh could not locate the airport in the dark. He soon found his landing spot and circled the area before his final descent:

In Expectant Wait

In Paris, *New York Times* reporter Edwin L. James described the crowd waiting at Le Bourget:

During a long, tense period no confirmation came. The people stood quietly, but the strain was becoming almost unbearable, . . . Pessimistic phrases were repeated. . . .

To these comments the inevitable reply was, "Don't give up hope. There's still time."

All this showed the French throng was unanimously eager for the American's safety and straining every wish for his ultimate victory.

A French woman dressed in mourning and sitting in a big limousine was seen wiping her eyes. . . . A woman selling papers near-by brushed her own tears aside exclaiming:

"You're right to feel so, madame. In such things there is no nationality—he's some mother's son."

. . . Soon after 9 o'clock this was turned to a cheering, shouting pandemonium when [Paris] Matin posted a bulletin announcing that the Lindbergh plane had been sighted over Cherbourg.[2]

I point the nose just short of the floodlights . . . I see the whole outline of the hangars, now. Two or three planes are resting in the shadows. . . . The lighted area is just ahead. It's barely large enough to land on. I nose down below the hangar roofs, so low that I can see the texture of the sod, and blades of grass on high spots. The ground is smooth and solid as far as the floodlights show its surface. I can tell nothing about the black mass beyond. Since Le Bourget is a major airport, the area between is probably also clear—I'll have to take a chance on that; if I land short, I may stop rolling before I reach it. [3]

"The *Spirit of St. Louis* is a wonderful plane. It's like a living creature, gliding along smoothly, happily, as though a successful flight means as much to it as to me, as though we shared our experiences together, each feeling beauty, life, and death as keenly, each dependent on the other's loyalty. *We* have made this flight across the ocean, not *I* or *it*." [4]

—*Charles Lindbergh, 1927*

Lindbergh landed in Paris at 10:22 p.m. on May 21, 1927. He had achieved his goal. When the *Spirit of St. Louis* rolled to a stop in the middle of Le Bourget, Lindbergh found that he was not alone. A crowd had eagerly been awaiting his arrival. The darkness that he thought was merely an empty field was actually full of people who frantically rushed toward him and his plane.

The Spirit of St. Louis *took off from Roosevelt Field on May 20, 1927.*

Crowds surrounded the Spirit of St. Louis *at Le Bourget airfield when it landed on May 21, 1927.*

LIFE IN THE SPOTLIGHT

"Lindbergh Does It!" the *New York Times* reported on its front page on May 22, 1927.[1] With his arrival at Le Bourget airfield 33.5 hours after departing New York, Charles Lindbergh secured a place in world history. He also won the hearts and admiration of countless people worldwide. The immediate response, however, came from the French. The thousands of people who had gathered in anticipation of the American's arrival rushed the field and mobbed Lindbergh. He described,

> *When my wheels touched earth, I had no way of knowing that tens of thousands of men and women were breaking down fences and flooding past guards.*

> *I had barely cut the engine switch when the first people reached my cockpit. Within seconds my open windows were blocked with faces. My name was called out over and over again, in accents strange to my ears—on this side of my plane—on that side—in front—in the distance.*[2]

Most Photographed

Charles Lindbergh's successful flight made him popular worldwide. Following his arrival in Paris, the aviator became the most photographed person in the world. During the first three weeks after his landing at Le Bourget, more than 7,430,000 feet (2,264,664 m) of newsreel film was taken of Lindbergh.

The force of all the people against the plane caused some of the wood to crack, while other people tore the fabric. After being carried away by the horde, Lindbergh was rescued by two French pilots. They took him to a hangar for safety and then to

meet the U.S. ambassador to France.
Souvenir hunters were going to tear
apart the *Spirit of St. Louis.* But the
plane was moved to a hangar and
rescued from the excited onlookers
who damaged the fuselage.

A HERO'S WELCOME

"Lucky Lindy," as Lindbergh
came to be called, left Paris on May
28, 1927. He headed home by way of
Belgium and England, where he was
greeted by more fans. In England,
the *Spirit of St. Louis* was taken apart and
packaged for shipping. After meeting
with British royalty and statesmen,
Lindbergh joined his dismantled
plane aboard the USS *Memphis* on
June 4 and headed for the United
States. He arrived in Washington
DC to a hero's welcome on June 11,
1927. His mother and U.S. President
Calvin Coolidge were in attendance.

During the reception, the
president gave a speech and presented

Honorary Doctorate

Although Charles Lind-
bergh did not complete his
studies at the University
of Wisconsin–Madison,
he did receive a degree.
A year after his successful
flight across the Atlantic,
the university granted the
second-year dropout an
honorary doctoral degree.

Lindbergh with the Distinguished Flying Cross. It is awarded "to any person who, while serving in any capacity with the Armed Forces of the United States, distinguishes himself by heroism or extraordinary achievement while participating in aerial flight."[3] In June, Lindbergh was granted lifetime membership in the National Aeronautic Association. When he visited New York City, Lindbergh was greeted with a ticker tape parade. During the welcoming ceremony, the mayor awarded the pilot with the Medal of Valor.

On June 16, Lindbergh received a check for $25,000 from Raymond Orteig. Lindbergh had met Orteig's challenge to become the first pilot to cross the Atlantic Ocean by plane. Finally, four weeks after reaching his goal, Lindbergh and the reassembled *Spirit of St. Louis* landed at Lambert Field in St. Louis on June 17. The city welcomed its adopted son with a parade the following day.

DEALING WITH FAME

Lindbergh's fame put him in contact with a variety of powerful people, including politicians and wealthy businessmen. Many seemed

Man of the Year

Time magazine named Charles Lindbergh its Man of the Year in 1927. It was the first time the magazine bestowed the honor, which has become a tradition for the publication. The new magazine did so in an attempt to increase its sales.

to want something from Lindbergh. Book publisher George Palmer Putnam convinced Lindbergh to share his story. The pilot wrote the 45,000-word tale, *We*, in only three weeks. His first royalty check was for $100,000.

Similar creative offers came that Lindbergh did not take. Newspaper publisher William Randolph Hearst wanted the flyer to star in a film about aviation. Hearst offered Lindbergh $500,000 and a royalty of 10 percent. Lindbergh was very tempted by the offer but ultimately

We

When Charles Lindbergh returned to the United States after his historic flight, newspaper and book publishers were eager to publish his story. The pilot agreed to let Putnam publish the tale of his New York–Paris flight.

Lindbergh agreed to have the book ghostwritten by Carlisle MacDonald. But the pilot changed his mind after reading the manuscript. He decided to write the book himself, promising a minimum of 40,000 words in three weeks. In his conclusion to *We*, Lindbergh wrote:

A description of my welcome back to the United States would, in itself, be sufficient to fill a larger volume than this. I am not an author by profession, and my pen could never express the gratitude which I feel towards the American people.

The voyage up the Potomac and to the Monument Grounds in Washington; up the Hudson River and along Broadway; over the Mississippi and to St. Louis—to do justice to these occasions would require a far greater writer than myself. Washington, New York, and finally St. Louis and home. Each of these cities has left me with an impression that I shall never forget, and a debt of gratitude which I can never repay.[4]

declined. He turned down other lucrative offers as well, including a second movie opportunity and a vaudeville request, both of which would have paid $1 million.

Lindbergh was a superstar. The world simply could not seem to get enough of him, and the attention quickly became overwhelming and dissatisfying for the quiet Midwesterner. He soon tired of the attention and lack of control over his life. He regained some control while still humoring the public as he embarked upon a 48-state tour.

FORTY-EIGHT STATES

Lindbergh met Harry Guggenheim in the summer of 1927. Guggenheim was a millionaire who loved aviation. He proposed an air tour of the United States. Lindbergh would use the tour to promote commercial aviation—and he could do it on his own terms. Lindbergh provided general input about the tour, then Guggenheim forged ahead with planning the specifics. After learning of the outline Guggenheim detailed, Lindbergh made two requests: the tour members must always be on time for the shows, and crowds must be controlled to avoid injury and damage.

The Lindy Hop

Dance marathons were popular during the time Charles Lindbergh flew to Paris from New York. In a dance marathon, couples danced together for hours to win prize money. At the end of one marathon, a contestant was asked by a reporter for the name of his dance. He called it the Lindy Hop. Lindy was a nickname for Lindbergh. Hop referred to his hop across the Atlantic.

Lindbergh and the *Spirit of St. Louis* landed in Hartford, Connecticut, on July 19 for the first stop in the trip. When the tour ended on October 23, 1927, in New York, Lindbergh had flown 22,350 miles (35,969 km), visited 82 cities, and visited each of the 48 states.

The tour had kept Lindbergh constantly on the move. He needed a vacation, which he took immediately. He spent a month in New Jersey resting before embarking on another trip. U.S. Ambassador to Mexico Dwight Morrow hoped that Lindbergh could improve relations with the United States' neighbor to the south. Lindbergh would fly another tour. This time, it would be 9,000 miles (14,484 km) in Latin America.

The end of the tour did not signal the end of Lindbergh's relationship with Morrow. Meeting Dwight Morrow would change Charles Lindbergh's life in ways he may never have imagined. ⌐

Charles Lindbergh with his mother, Evangeline, in 1927

Charles Lindbergh and Anne Morrow

MARRIAGE, FAMILY, AND LOSS

In his business dealings with Ambassador Morrow, Charles Lindbergh came to know Morrow's family, including his daughter, Anne. Anne Morrow was a quiet, introspective, blue-eyed girl with dark hair. She was also an avid writer.

When she graduated from high school in 1924, Anne was at the top of her class, student council president, and captain of the field hockey team. Given her love of writing, it was no surprise that she also contributed to the school's literary magazine.

Anne next studied at Smith College, a private women's college in Northampton, Massachusetts. She majored in English literature and also took courses in creative writing. She was attending Smith when news came of Lindbergh's successful flight across the Atlantic. Seven months later, she met the world-famous pilot when her parents entertained him in Mexico for a week during the Christmas holiday. Both of the young people were smitten.

The couple began dating shortly thereafter and fell in love. Anne graduated from Smith in 1928. In November 1928, Lindbergh proposed. On May 27, 1929, Charles Lindbergh and Anne Morrow married.

A LIFE TOGETHER

Given his status and celebrity as a pilot, Lindbergh had received many job offers. He decided to work for Pan American Airways and Transcontinental Air Transport. In addition to flying for the companies, he served as a technical consultant. After the couple married, Anne joined her husband in his work. She would soon join him in his passion for flying. She would also soon share with him a role neither had held before—that of parent.

Charles Augustus Lindbergh Jr. was born on June 22, 1930, on Anne's twenty-fourth birthday. The couple moved into a rented farmhouse in Princeton, New Jersey, while Lindbergh began building a house for his family in Hopewell, New Jersey.

HEADING EAST

The year 1930 was monumental for Anne in another way—she earned a glider pilot's license. She was the first woman in the United States to do so. Anne and Charles Lindbergh became flying partners. She was his copilot, navigator, and radio operator. In 1931, Lindbergh

The Wedding

When Charles Lindbergh and Anne Morrow married, there was such an intense media interest in the couple that the event was kept a secret, even from those attending. Anne's mother hosted an informal party that included the minister of the Morrows' church. Mrs. Morrow wove her way through her crowd of guests and asked them to go to the living room and stand when the minister stood. They did, and then a side door to the room opened. Anne was in a wedding dress. The couple married, changed their clothes, and drove to Long Island, where they boarded a boat named *Mouette* and eventually reached their honeymoon destination in Maine.

decided to fly to Asia to determine the best air routes for Pan American. The couple completed the three-month journey together, traveling to Canada, Alaska, Russia, and China. The two shared both a marriage and a love of flying.

North to the Orient

Anne Morrow Lindbergh's three-month journey with her husband to China in 1931 was the subject of her first book. Published in 1935, *North to the Orient* was an instant success.

FAMILY LOSSES

The Lindberghs completed their flight in Asia on October 2, 1931. Three days later, they received sad news. Dwight Morrow, Anne's father, had died from a stroke. The unexpected death of the 58-year-old left the family in shock.

The following March, the family was thrown again into a horrific situation. Lindbergh and his wife and child were at home on the evening of March 1, 1932, along with Betty Gow, the baby's nurse. Lindbergh heard a noise, but thought nothing of it. Later that evening, when Gow went to check on the baby, she was terrified to find him gone. Twenty-month-old Charles Jr. had been kidnapped.

Once again, Lindbergh was in newspaper headlines. The newspapers printed a letter from the Lindberghs to the culprit, asking for the safe return of their son. But this was to no avail. Baby Charles was found dead in a shallow grave on May 12, 1932.

Moving On

While the Lindberghs were dealing with the disappearance and death of their first child, they were also preparing for their second. Jon was born on August 16, 1932. Also during this time, Charles Lindbergh was pursuing a new venture.

Lindbergh was an innovative pilot, but his skills with airplane mechanics translated to other areas. In the 1930s, Lindbergh collaborated with heart surgeon Alexis Carrel on an experiment. The two men had met in 1930. At that time, Elisabeth Morrow, Anne's sister, was having medical problems because of heart illness and required surgery. Her doctor told Lindbergh such a surgery could not be performed, because it would require stopping the heart too long. Lindbergh envisioned a pump that would reside outside the body and keep the heart going while surgery was performed. Carrel had been attempting such an apparatus. The two partnered to work toward their common goal.

While Lindbergh worked with Carrel and continued to care for his wife and new son, investigators continued to search for baby Charles's killer. Bruno Richard Hauptmann, a German immigrant who worked as a carpenter, was formally charged with the crime in late 1934. On February 14, 1935, he was found guilty by a jury.

By this time, Charles Lindbergh had experienced enough of the spotlight. He decided it was time to leave his homeland. He explained to Deac Lyman, a reporter for the *New York Times*, "I've got to get Anne and the baby away. Crank

Crime of the Century

As was often the case since Lindbergh completed the first transatlantic flight, media around him created a circus-like atmosphere. When his son was kidnapped on March 1, 1932, the case was deemed the "Crime of the Century" by the media.

Charles and Anne Lindbergh looked to the media for help with finding their son. Leading newspapers included a letter from the couple to the kidnappers. In it, the Lindberghs asked for the child's return in exchange for no risk of charges:

We urge those who have the child to select any representatives of ours who will be suitable to them at any time and at any place that they may designate.
If this is accepted, we promise that we will keep whatever arrangements that may be made by their representative and ours strictly confidential and we further pledge ourselves that we will not try to injure in any way those connected with the return of the child.[1]

The letter was of no use in the case. The baby was found dead and partially buried less than five miles (8 km) from the Lindbergh home. Bruno Richard Hauptmann was found guilty of the crime and sentenced to death. On April 3, 1936, Hauptmann was put to death by electrocution.

letters have started again. There have been threats against the family. I'm going to make England my home."[2]

The Lindberghs set sail for a new home on a new continent. Lindbergh was proceeding with his life, but the end of an era had come. Lindbergh was no longer only "Lucky Lindy." He was a husband and a father looking out for his family. He was also an American, and his aviation expertise would soon help the U.S. government. However, his political views regarding the United States would also taint the shining image that many around the world held of the record-making pilot. ⌐

Retiring His Plane

In the spring of 1928, Charles Lindbergh retired the *Spirit of St. Louis*. He donated his beloved airplane to the Smithsonian Institution in Washington DC, where it is still on display.

Anne and son Jon at their home in Long Barn, England, in the 1930s

Charles Lindbergh, in goggles, arrived in Germany in 1938 for a meeting about aviation research.

WORLD WAR II

After moving to England, Charles Lindbergh was invited to France to visit the country's aircraft plants. Next, the U.S. military attaché in Berlin, Germany, Truman Smith, arranged approval for Lindbergh to inspect

Germany's aircraft industry. Smith
had noticed the country's growing
air force and was concerned.
Adolf Hitler had assumed power
in Germany in 1933 and his Nazi
regime was growing. A military man,
Smith was familiar with land fighting.
He wanted an aviation expert to assess
Germany's flying power.

"We are very happy in England. At least we are able to read and think about things which are both pleasant and interesting."[2]

—*Charles Lindbergh*

Visiting Germany

The Lindberghs arrived in Berlin on July 22,
1936, for a weeklong visit. Lindbergh visited a
number of bases and airplane factories. He also flew
some German planes. During his visit, Lindbergh
gave a speech to a group of aviators and diplomats
in which he presented a new side of himself that was
reminiscent of his politically minded father. He
reminded his audience of the importance of peace
and the responsibility held by those who fly, saying,

*Aviation has brought a revolutionary change to a world
already staggering from changes. It is our responsibility to
make sure that in doing so we do not destroy the very things
which we wish to protect.*[1]

He later noted:

I tried to issue a warning of the dangers involved in the Nazi military development, and, at the same time, keep in mind that I was a guest of Germany on an invitation issued through the military branch of an American Embassy.[3]

Although Lindbergh was concerned about Germany's growing military force and the situation Jews were beginning to face, he and Anne were also taken with the country. The couple was impressed by all that Adolf Hitler had done to improve the German economy since World War I. Both could see Hitler's fanaticism, but they believed him to be a great leader.

Lindbergh warned others of Germany's growing military air power. During his second trip, in 1937, he saw how much the Luftwaffe, Germany's air force, had grown since his previous visit. He also knew that air power in England, France, and the United States was not growing at nearly the same pace. Lindbergh began to explore air forces in other European countries, including

Another Son

After moving to England, Anne Lindbergh gave birth to the couple's third child, a son. Land Morrow Lindbergh was born on May 12, 1937. Unlike Anne's previous two pregnancies, the public was not made aware of her third.

Czechoslovakia, Poland, Romania, and the Soviet Union.

During a visit to the Soviet Union in 1937, Lindbergh assessed its air power as inferior to Germany's. The Soviets took the remark as a sign that Lindbergh was not grateful for the hospitality he and Anne had been shown during their visit. A U.S. newspaper reported that Lindbergh was pro-Nazi.

Lindbergh visited Germany a third time in October 1938. During a dinner at the U.S. embassy, Hermann Goering, Hitler's top assistant, gave Lindbergh the Service Cross of the German Eagle for his aviation work and record-making flight to Paris. This was a high civilian honor. A few weeks after receiving the medal, on November 9, 1938, anti-Semitic riots broke out in Germany. Following the story of the violence against German Jews, U.S. newspapers criticized Lindbergh for not returning the medal.

Kristallnacht

Kristallnacht refers to November 9, 1938. In the evening, Jewish synagogues and other buildings throughout Germany were vandalized by Nazis. Hitler's storm troopers also attacked Jews. By night's end, the Jews in Germany suffered terrible losses: 7,000 businesses and 900 synagogues were damaged or destroyed. There were 91 deaths among the Jews, and as many as 30,000 Jews were sent to concentration camps. This was the beginning of Adolf Hitler's attempt to eradicate Jews. *Kristallnacht* is a German word that translates literally to "crystal night." The common English translation is "night of broken glass."

Lindbergh visited Germany again in late 1938 and early 1939. Traveling alone, the American arranged for France's purchase of engines to install in French aircraft. The Lindberghs had moved to France in late 1937, and Lindbergh was working with the French to improve their fighter planes. The negotiation went well, but the deal was never completed. When Germany invaded Czechoslovakia in early 1939, the arrangement was cancelled. Negotiations were off, and another world war was on the horizon.

Throughout the late 1930s, Lindbergh gathered important information for U.S. intelligence. He shared his assessments of the air power of Germany, England, France, the Soviet Union, and other nations with U.S. diplomats and politicians. In the fall of 1938, he expressed to Joseph P. Kennedy, the U.S. ambassador to England, his concerns about the military forces of certain countries. Lindbergh foresaw war in Europe and wanted it avoided. The aviator believed civilization would be destroyed.

America First

In 1939, the Lindberghs anticipated war in Europe and moved back to the United States.

Upon his return, Lindbergh agreed to work for the air corps and the National Advisory Committee for Aeronautics, which aided the development of U.S. military air defense. Lindbergh also began sharing his European observations and experiences publicly. He shared his belief that the United States should not get involved in the conflict in Europe.

Nazi Germany invaded Poland on September 1, 1939, and Britain and France declared war on Germany two days later. Lindbergh gave his first speech regarding the war in Europe on September 15, 1939, in a nationwide radio broadcast. He urged the United States not to become involved in the war, particularly because it would result in the loss of millions of American lives. Lindbergh opposed President Franklin D. Roosevelt, who did his best to aid Great Britain and the Soviet Union in their war efforts.

Lindbergh's views were not well received by everyone. Some people called him pro-German. The English

A Girl Joins the Family

While Lindbergh was busy opposing President Roosevelt and trying to keep the United States out of the war in Europe, Anne was busy supporting her husband. She was also preparing for the birth of her fourth child. Anne Spencer Lindbergh was born on October 2, 1940. She was called "Ansy" to help avoid confusion because she and her mother shared the same name.

were astonished by Lindbergh's lack of concern for
them, especially after he had lived in England. While
Lindbergh was voicing his view to the United States,
a group formed an organization that was isolationist
in nature. It was named for its position: America
First Committee. Lindbergh joined the group in
April 1941 and continued to share his opinion in
speeches and in print regarding President Roosevelt
and the war.

Roosevelt was frustrated by Lindbergh and
expressed his feelings about the pilot during a press
conference on April 25, 1941. Roosevelt questioned
Lindbergh's loyalty as an American and a member
of the U.S. Army Air Corps when he was so opposed
to the viewpoints of his commander in chief. In
response, Lindbergh resigned his commission.

In September, Lindbergh gave a speech in
Des Moines, Iowa, that upset many. Lindbergh
named some groups that he believed were pushing
the United States into war, including Jews. The
speech garnered criticism from a variety of people,
including members of America First, but the group
did not publicly scold or disown him. Rather, it
issued a statement that Lindbergh and America First
were not anti-Semitic. The group continued to

promote its cause, but Lindbergh's speech in Iowa caused irreparable harm to his reputation and the organization.

On December 7, 1941, the Japanese attacked Pearl Harbor, Hawaii. The United States was now at war, and the policies pushed for by America First were null and void.

Aiding the War Effort

Once the United States entered World War II, Lindbergh withdrew his isolationist stance. His country had been attacked, and the aviator

The America First Committee

The America First Committee was founded in 1940. The organization grew to approximately 800,000 members, including businessmen, clergymen, and politicians.

The group wrote a letter of introduction that included a list of their beliefs:

1. *The United States must build an impregnable defense for America.*
2. *No foreign power, nor group of powers, can successfully attack a prepared America.*
3. *American democracy can be preserved only by keeping out of the European War.*
4. *Aid short of war weakens national defense at home and threatens to involve America in war abroad.[4]*

A few days after the Japanese attacked Pearl Harbor, the America First Committee issued the following statement:

We are at war . . . the primary objective is . . . victory. Therefore, the America First Committee has determined immediately to cease all functions and to dissolve as soon as that can legally be done. And finally, it urges all those who have followed its lead to give their full support to the war effort of the nation, until peace is attained.[5]

wanted to take action. Because he had resigned his commission in the air corps, Lindbergh had to reenlist to fly in the military. His request to rejoin was declined.

But Lindbergh would find another way to help the war effort. Automobile pioneer Henry Ford hired Lindbergh to work at an assembly plant that manufactured B-24 bombers. In addition to providing his expertise in airplane design, Lindbergh also served as a test pilot.

In 1944, Lindbergh finally was able to fly as a fighter pilot—a role he had trained for but never had the chance to take on. The opportunity came from United Aircraft, which hired him as a technical advisor. The company sent Lindbergh to the Pacific and placed him under the supervision of the U.S. Navy. The experienced aviator helped pilots drastically increase fuel efficiency. In addition, Lindbergh flew 50 combat missions, even though he was not in the military. —

Charles Lindbergh, right, aided the U.S. military during World War II by inspecting aircraft.

Throughout their marriage, Anne often flew alongside Charles and served as his copilot.

THE LATER YEARS

ollowing World War II, Charles Lindbergh led a quieter life that was out of the public eye. He and Anne were now the parents of five children. Anne Spencer, known as Ansy, had been born in 1940, and Scott arrived in the early morning of August 13, 1943. Two years later, after Anne had believed her childbearing years were over, the couple welcomed a second daughter. Reeve was born on October 2, 1945. She shared her birthday with her sister, Ansy.

Lindbergh was now in his forties. During this time, his family settled down in Westport, Connecticut. In many ways, Lindbergh was a good father to his children. He played games with them and read to them, but he could also be overly demanding. One of Jon's schoolteachers wrote of her pupil's father, "The children like him, but are puzzled by his dreaminess, abruptness, and periodic indifference to them when he is involved in his own plans."[1]

Anne struggled with Lindbergh as well. He had expectations of her just as he had of the children. She was charged with keeping detailed accounts of household finances and inventories. He also

Anne's Books

Anne Lindbergh wrote several books, including autobiographies, nonfiction, fiction, and poetry:
- *North to the Orient* (1935)
- *Listen! The Wind* (1938)
- *The Wave of the Future, a Confession of Faith* (1940)
- *The Steep Ascent* (1944)
- *Gift from the Sea* (1955)
- *The Unicorn, and Other Poems, 1935–1955* (1956)
- *Bring Me a Unicorn* (1972)
- *Hour of Gold, Hour of Lead* (1973)
- *Locked Rooms and Open Doors* (1974)
- *The Flower and the Nettle* (1976)
- *War Within and Without* (1980)

pressured her to write, which was challenging at times because of writer's block. She realized how little her husband understood or communicated with her. At times, she would end up alone crying. Betty Morrow, Anne's mother, wrote of the situation at her daughter's house: "The atmosphere—the tension in the house is so terrible—that when C. goes off for a day or two—everybody sings!"[2] The house was merely a place for Anne and the children to stay while Lindbergh continued to follow his pursuits.

LINDBERGH THE AUTHOR

Awards

After the war, Charles Lindbergh was awarded two of the aviation world's highest honors. In 1949, he was granted the Wright Brothers Memorial Trophy. In 1954, he received the Daniel Guggenheim Medal for his "pioneering achievement in flight and air navigation."[3]

Later in 1954, Lindbergh received another honor. On April 7, he was sworn in as Brigadier General Charles Lindbergh.

Charles Lindbergh had begun recording the events of his life—the everyday and the monumental—when he was only a boy. After his successful New York–Paris flight, he became an author with the publication of *We* in 1927. Lindbergh's second book, *Of Flight and Life*, was published on August 23, 1948. A reflection on his experiences and thoughts, its initial printing of 10,000 copies sold out in one day. An additional 40,000 copies of the book were printed and sold out in a matter of weeks. The book was a popular and critical success.

Lindbergh's *Of Flight and Life* put him back in the hearts of thousands of Americans, but his next title brought him even more success. Although it had sold well, Lindbergh had not been pleased with *We*. He decided to rewrite the autobiography of his historic flight. After extensive writing, rewriting, and editing, *The Spirit of St. Louis* was published in 1953. The 600-page book was a sales success and received critical acclaim. In spring 1954, Lindbergh received the prestigious Pulitzer Prize. Like his wife, he had become a successful author.

CONSULTANT AND ADVISOR

When he was not writing or attending to other matters, Lindbergh continued consulting and advising, just as he had done so many times during and before the war. Although he was not a member of the U.S. Air Force, Lindbergh was a consultant for that branch's chief of staff. He visited U.S. air bases worldwide, including those in Alaska, Europe, Japan, and the Philippines.

Lindbergh also spent considerable time working for Pan American. Sometimes, he attended meetings in New York City, but the position also allowed him to travel extensively to inspect airliners and facilities around the globe. Throughout the 1950s, he traveled the world.

REFLECTING

In the 1960s, Lindbergh began to speak out publicly about his concern for the environment. Lindbergh became a member of the World Wildlife Fund, the International Union for the Conservation of Nature, and the Nature Conservancy. He was particularly burdened by the effects of new technologies on natural habitats. He worried that human actions and pollution would destroy wildlife. Although he had stayed out of the spotlight for many years, Lindbergh helped establish a national park in Minnesota.

As Lindbergh continued to fly around the world for Pan American, he penned another book. He wrote parts of it while in various locations, including the Philippines,

Space Enthusiast

Charles Lindbergh was interested in and involved with the U.S. space program. Lindbergh helped raise funds for Robert H. Goddard, a rocket researcher who foresaw space exploration.

Neil Armstrong, the famous American astronaut, viewed Lindbergh as one of his heroes. Armstrong first met Lindbergh at the launch of Apollo 8, in which astronauts orbited the moon and returned safely to Earth. Lindbergh was also invited to the launch of Apollo 11, the first mission in which astronauts walked on the moon.

Charles Lindbergh visited Voyageurs National Park in Minnesota in 1969. Lindbergh was an advocate for environmental preservation.

Germany, and the United States. This book focused on the aviator's youth. *Boyhood on the Upper Mississippi: A Reminiscent Letter* was published by the Minnesota Historical Society in 1972.

Lindbergh also worked with the society on a project in his home state: the Lindbergh Historic Site. The Little Falls house in which Lindbergh grew up became a historic site. The house and the land on which it stands are maintained in honor of his political father. Lindbergh helped the society in the creation and accuracy of its exhibit. He also attended its opening ceremony in 1973.

FINAL STOP

There were more personal challenges ahead for Lindbergh. During a physical examination, Lindbergh's doctor found a lump that turned out to be cancer. The famous flyer received three days of radiation treatment at a hospital in New

---

A Daughter Remembers

In 2002, the Minnesota Historical Society Press released an updated version of *Lindbergh Looks Back: A Boyhood Reminiscence*. The book includes a foreword by Reeve Lindbergh, the youngest Lindbergh child. In the foreword, Reeve wrote of her father:

He was a man who loved his family and who loved his country, too, in a way that seems old-fashioned to many people now, but that comes naturally enough to those who know the country very well from earliest childhood, with a physical as well as an emotional understanding. When his life became more complicated than he ever had wished it or expected it to be, he was able to reach back to that understanding, to an affection for the earth he had known and experienced in his childhood, combined with a never-ending fascination for the land he had flown over as a young pilot, and the world he came to know internationally, as an older pilot. This love for the living earth, and for life itself, was his earliest strength, second only to his association with my mother in its intensity, and strong enough that it sustained him all the way through the very last days of his life.[4]

York City in late January and early February 1973. Charles and Anne Lindbergh had purchased land and built a home in Hawaii in 1969, and Lindbergh chose to rest and recover there.

Also in February of that year, Lindbergh turned 72. He could no longer fly for Pan American because of the company's mandatory retirement age of 72. In June, he experienced a high fever caused by his cancer, which was spreading. He spent a month in a New York hospital. Trips planned to Switzerland and Minnesota were canceled. He was readmitted to the hospital on July 24 only to learn that the doctors could do nothing more for him. On August 14, Lindbergh met with William Jovanovich, an editor and publisher. They discussed a memoir Lindbergh had been writing. Jovanovich believed the 400 pages he had read were good enough to publish and signed a contract with Lindbergh, who then provided another 1,000 pages.

Two days later, on August 16, Lindbergh insisted on returning to Hawaii to die. He made detailed

More Than One Family

In November 2003, the British Broadcasting Corporation (BBC) confirmed that Charles Lindbergh had fathered children outside his marriage. He had three children with a German hatmaker named Brigitte Hesshaimer.

According to other sources, Lindbergh allegedly fathered two more children with the woman's sister, Marietta Hesshaimer. Supposedly, he also had two children with his secretary, a woman named Valeska.

plans for his service, memorial, and burial. Charles Lindbergh died on August, 26, 1974, at the age of 72 years. He was buried at the cemetery of the Palapala Ho'omau Church in Hawaii.

REMEMBERING LINDBERGH

Regardless of his political beliefs and speeches, or how his behavior affected his wife and children, there is no denying Lindbergh's influence on aviation. He was one of the most famous people of the twentieth century and possibly the first media star—regardless of whether he wanted to be.

Final Book

The manuscript that Charles Lindbergh gave William Jovanovich in 1974 became the pilot's last book. *Autobiography of Values* was published in 1978. In it, Lindbergh wrote, "After my death, the molecules of my being will return to the earth and the sky. They came from the stars. I am of the stars."[5]

Lindbergh created limitless possibilities for himself doing the work he loved: flying. As a young man in college, he realized that he wanted to be a pilot and actively pursued that goal. For many, such a life would have remained only a dream. For Charles Lindbergh, it was a reality that forever made him "Lucky Lindy," the first pilot to successfully complete a transatlantic flight.

Charles Lindbergh left an indelible mark on aviation history.

TIMELINE

1902	1906	1912
Charles Augustus Lindbergh is born on February 4.	Lindbergh's father is elected to U.S. Congress.	Lindbergh attends his first air show.

1922	1924	1925
Lindbergh flies as a passenger in an airplane for the first time in April.	Lindbergh joins the Army Air Corps Reserve.	Lindbergh graduates first in his class from the U.S. Air Service Flying School.

1918	1920	1922
Lindbergh graduates from high school.	Lindbergh starts attending college at the University of Wisconsin–Madison.	Lindbergh drops out of college.

1927	1927	1928
Lindbergh takes off from Roosevelt Field in New York on May 20.	Lindbergh arrives at Le Bourget airport in Paris on May 21.	Lindbergh donates the *Spirit of St. Louis* plane to the Smithsonian Institution.

TIMELINE

1929	1932	1935–1939
Lindbergh marries Anne Morrow on May 27.	Charles A. Lindbergh Jr. is kidnapped on March 1. The baby is found dead on May 12.	Lindbergh lives in Europe to escape the U.S. spotlight.

1944	1953	1954
Lindbergh conducts 50 combat missions in the Pacific.	Lindbergh's *The Spirit of St. Louis* is published.	Lindbergh is awarded the Pulitzer Prize for *The Spirit of St. Louis*.

1936–1938

Lindbergh assesses the military air power of Germany and other European nations.

1940–1941

Lindbergh promotes isolationism.

1941

Lindbergh speaks against U.S. involvement in World War II as part of America First.

1974

Lindbergh dies on August 26.

1977

The Lindbergh House is designated a National Historic Landmark.

Essential Facts

Date of Birth
February 4, 1902

Place of Birth
Detroit, Michigan

Date of Death
August 26, 1974

Parents
Charles August "C. A." Lindbergh and Evangeline Lodge Land
Lindbergh

Education

Force School; Sidwell Friends School; Little Falls High School;
University of Wisconsin—Madison; Lincoln Standard Aircraft

Marriage

Anne Morrow Lindbergh (May 27, 1929)

Children

With Anne: Charles Augustus Lindbergh Jr., Jon Morrow
Lindbergh, Land Morrow Lindbergh, Anne Spencer Lindbergh,
Scott Morrow Lindbergh, Reeve Lindbergh

With Brigitte Hesshaimer: Dyrk Hesshaimer, Astrid Bouteuil, and
David Hesshaimer

Career Highlights

Lindbergh completed the first successful nonstop, solo transatlantic flight. He also gathered information about German military holdings for the United States. Lindbergh authored many books and won the Pulitzer Prize.

Societal Contribution

Charles Lindbergh ignited interest in aviation with his transatlantic flight from New York to Paris in 1927. He also helped to advance aviation for commercial and military use.

Conflicts

During the late 1930s and early 1940s, Lindbergh repeatedly expressed his belief that the United States should not become involved in the war in Europe. He and President Franklin D. Roosevelt held opposing viewpoints and clashed on the matter.

Quote

"Why shouldn't I fly from New York to Paris? I'm almost twenty-five, I have more than four years of aviation behind me, and close to two thousand hours in the air. . . . I've flown my mail through the worst of nights. I know the wind currents of the Rocky Mountains and the storms of the Mississippi Valley as few pilots know them. During my year at Brooks and Kelly as a flying cadet, I learned the basic elements of navigation. . . . Why am I not qualified for such a flight?" —*Charles Lindbergh*

ADDITIONAL RESOURCES

SELECT BIBLIOGRAPHY

Berg, A. Scott. *Lindbergh*. New York, NY: Penguin Putnam, 1998.

Lindbergh, Charles A. *Lindbergh Looks Back: A Boyhood Reminiscence*. St. Paul, MN: Minnesota Historical Society Press, 2002.

Lindbergh, Charles A. *The Spirit of St. Louis*. New York, NY: Charles Scribner's Sons, 1953.

Ross, Walter S. *The Last Hero: Charles A. Lindbergh*. New York, NY: Harper & Row, 1968.

FURTHER READING

Charles Lindbergh Graphic Biography. Irvine, CA: Saddleback Educational Publishing, 2008.

Giblin, James Cross. *Charles A. Lindbergh: A Human Hero*. New York, NY: Clarion, 1997.

Lindbergh, Charles A. *We*. New York, NY: Putnam and Sons, 1927.

Raatma, Lucia. *Charles Lindbergh: Pilot*. Chicago, IL: Ferguson Publishing Company, 2000.

WEB LINKS

To learn more about Charles Lindbergh, visit ABDO Publishing Company online at **www.abdopublishing.com**. Web sites about Charles Lindbergh are featured on our Book Links page. These links are routinely monitored and updated to provide the most current information available.

Places to Visit

Charles A. Lindbergh Historic Site
1620 Lindbergh Drive South, Little Falls, MN 56345
320-616-5421
www.mnhs.org/places/sites/lh/
The Charles A. Lindbergh Historic Site provides the full scope of Lindbergh's life, beginning with his boyhood along the Mississippi in Little Falls, MN. His childhood home and exhibits are part of the site, which is a National Historic Landmark operated by the Minnesota Historical Society.

Charles A. Lindbergh State Park
1615 Lindbergh Drive South, Little Falls, MN 56345
320-616-2525
www.dnr.state.mn.us/state_parks/charles_a_lindbergh/index.html
The park is located on the Mississippi River in central Minnesota, just southwest of Little Falls. The park offers hiking and skiing trails, a picnic area, and a wooded campground.

Smithsonian Institution, National Air and Space Museum
National Mall Building, Independence Avenue at Sixth Street Southwest, Washington, DC 20560
202-633-1000
www.nasm.si.edu/museum/flagship.cfm
www.nasm.si.edu/exhibitions/gal100/gal100.html (online exhibit)
Charles Lindbergh's historic plane, *Spirit of St. Louis*, is on display at the Milestones of Flight exhibition, which highlights aircraft and spacecraft. The exhibit also includes the Wright brothers' 1903 Wright Flyer, the first American jet, and the command module from the first lunar landing mission.

Glossary

anti-Semitism
Hostility toward Jews.

attaché
A government employee specializing in a particular topic who is stationed at an office in another country.

backer
Someone who provides financial support for a project.

barnstormer
A pilot or aerialist who travels to perform aerial tricks for money.

bond
Money paid as insurance when using something. The money is returned to the person using an item if that item is returned safely.

crown
In dentistry, an artificial exterior that replaces the enamel of a tooth.

embezzle
To steal something, such as money, that is entrusted to one's care.

fanaticism
Enthusiasm or beliefs that are extreme and sometimes irrational.

fuselage
The body of an airplane.

ghostwrite
When a paid, professional writer writes for another person, usually a famous person who is not a writer.

handbill
A paper printed with an advertisement.

immigrant
Someone who has moved to a country from another one.

impregnable
Too strong to be captured or entered by force.

isolationist
One who believes keeping his or her country separate from other countries politically and economically is the best course of action.

monoplane
A plane with a single pair of wings.

prospectus
The description of a plan, such as a business; it is used to attract backers.

royalty
A portion of the profit from each book sold.

tenant
A person who lives temporarily at a farm to work on it.

widower
A man whose wife has died.

wing walker
During the barnstorming era of the 1920s, a person who performed aerial tricks such as walking on an airplane's wings while it was in flight.

Source Notes

Chapter 1. Risky Journey
1. Charles A. Lindbergh. *The Spirit of St. Louis.* New York, NY: Charles Scribner's Sons, 1953. 15.
2. Ibid.

Chapter 2. Young Charles
1. Charles A. Lindbergh. *Lindbergh Looks Back: A Boyhood Reminiscence.* St. Paul, MN: Historical Society Press, 2002. 13.
2. A. Scott Berg. *Lindbergh.* New York, NY: Penguin Putnam, 1998. 41.
3. Ibid. 43.

Chapter 3. Dreaming of Flight
1. Charles A. Lindbergh. *Lindbergh Looks Ba k: A Boyhood Reminiscence.* St. Paul, MN: Historical Society Press, 2002. 53.
2. Ibid.
3. A. Scott Berg. *Lindbergh.* New York, NY: Penguin Putnam, 1998. 56.
4. Ibid. 58.
5. Charles A. Lindbergh. *Lindbergh Looks Back: A Boyhood Reminiscence.* St. Paul, MN: Historical Society Press, 2002. 53.
6. A. Scott Berg. *Lindbergh.* New York, NY: Penguin Putnam, 1998. 63.

Chapter 4. Finally, a Pilot
1. A. Scott Berg. *Lindbergh.* New York, NY: Penguin Putnam, 1998. 70.
2. Ibid. 71.

Chapter 5. Working as a Flyer
1. Walter S. Ross. *The Last Hero: Charles A. Lindbergh.* New York, NY: Harper & Row, 1968. 70.
2. Ibid. 71.
3. A. Scott Berg. *Lindbergh.* New York, NY: Penguin Putnam, 1998. 89.
4. Charles A. Lindbergh. *The Spirit of St. Louis.* New York, NY: Charles Scribner's Sons, 1953. 14, 15.

Chapter 6. New York to Paris
1. A. Scott Berg. *Lindbergh*. New York, NY: Penguin Putnam, 1998. 95.
2. Edwin L. James. "Lindbergh Does It! To Paris in 33 1/2 Hours; Flies 1,000 Miles Through Snow and Sleet; Cheering French Carry Him Off Field." *New York Times*. 22 May 1927. *Charleslindbergh. com.* 2007. 23 Aug. 2009 <http://www.charleslindbergh.com/ny/1. asp>.
3. Charles A. Lindbergh. *The Spirit of St. Louis.* New York, NY: Charles Scribner's Sons, 1953. 490.
4. Ibid. 486.

Chapter 7. Life in the Spotlight
1. Edwin L. James. "Lindbergh Does It! To Paris in 33 1/2 Hours; Flies 1,000 Miles Through Snow and Sleet; Cheering French Carry Him Off Field." *New York Times*. 22 May 1927. *Charleslindbergh. com.* 2007. 23 Aug. 2009 <http://www.charleslindbergh.com/ny/1. asp>.
2. Charles A. Lindbergh. *The Spirit of St. Louis.* New York, NY: Charles Scribner's Sons, 1953. 495.
3. "Distinguished Flying Cross." *Gruntsmilitary.com.* 23 Aug. 2009 <http://www.gruntsmilitary.com/dfc.shtml>.
4. Charles A. Lindbergh. *We.* New York, NY: Putnam, 1927. 230.

Chapter 8. Marriage, Family, and Loss
1. Walter S. Ross. *The Last Hero: Charles A. Lindbergh.* New York, NY: Harper & Row, 1968. 200.
2. Ibid. 224.

Source Notes Continued

Chapter 9. World War II
1. A. Scott Berg. *Lindbergh*. New York, NY: Penguin Putnam, 1998. 358.
2. Ibid. 352.
3. Ibid. 358.
4. Ibid. 411.
5. Walter S. Ross. *The Last Hero: Charles A. Lindbergh*. New York, NY: Harper & Row, 1968. 315.

Chapter 10. The Later Years
1. A. Scott Berg. *Lindbergh*. New York, NY: Penguin Putnam, 1998. 480.
2. Ibid.
3. Ibid. 487.
4. Charles A. Lindbergh. *Lindbergh Looks Back: A Boyhood Reminiscence*. St. Paul, MN: Historical Society Press, 2002. vii.
5. "New Concerns, Final Days." *PBS*. 25 Aug. 2009 <http://www.pbs.org/wgbh/amex/lindbergh/sfeature/final.html>.

INDEX

Index

ABOUT THE AUTHOR

Rebecca Rowell has a Master of Arts in Publishing and Writing from Emerson College. She has edited numerous nonfiction children's books, including several biographies. Born and raised in Minneapolis, Minnesota, she has lived in Arizona, Massachusetts, and Austria. She once again lives in Minneapolis, where she enjoys arranging flowers when she is not editing, writing, or spending time with her cats.

PHOTO CREDITS